A BABY IN THE HOUSE

"I'm Jasmine, your sister."

Sophie let loose an ear-piercing scream. Jasmine couldn't believe that someone so small could make such a horrible sound.

"I was just trying to be nice," Jasmine said.

"It's probably her diaper," Mrs. James said. "It must need changing."

"Let me do that," said Mr. James, rushing forward.

Mrs. James gave Mr. James the baby. The nurse-midwife rushed over with a package of baby wipes. Mr. James laid Sophie on the changing table and unwrapped her clothes. Inside was a tiny body with wiggling arms and legs.

Sophie let out a yell. She waved her fists and kicked her feet. Her face turned purple with rage.

Sophie might be little, Jasmine thought, but she sure knew how to get attention.

Pony Tails

Jasmine Helps a Foal

B O N N I E   B R Y A N T

Illustrated by Marcy Ramsey

A SKYLARK BOOK
NEW YORK • TORONTO • LONDON • SYDNEY • AUCKLAND

RL 3, 007–010
JASMINE HELPS A FOAL
A Bantam Skylark Book / November 1996

ISBN 0-553-48383-8

Published simultaneously in the United States and Canada.

Bantam Books are published by Bantam Books, a division of Bantam
Doubleday Dell Publishing Group, Inc. Its trademark, consisting of the
words "Bantam Books" and the portrayal of a rooster, is Registered in
U.S. Patent and Trademark Office and in other countries. Marca
Registrada. Bantam Books, 1540 Broadway, New York, New York 10036.

PRINTED IN THE UNITED STATES OF AMERICA

OPM   0   9   8   7   6   5   4   3   2   1

*I would like to give my special thanks
to Helen Geraghty for her help
in the writing of this book.*

Jasmine
Helps a Foal

1 A Growing Family

"Will you slow down, May?" said Corey.

"I think I'll go faster," May said. She urged her pony into a flat-out gallop.

"Stop!" Jasmine said.

"Watch this!" May said. Her pony jumped the ruler, and then the eraser, and then Jasmine's diary.

Corey and Jasmine looked at each other and rolled their eyes. These model ponies were turning May into a maniac.

"It's good to ride safely at all times," Corey said, but then she giggled. "Even if your pony is only six inches tall."

Corey jumped her model pony over a fuzzy bedroom slipper and up onto the window seat.

1

"Your turn," Corey said to Jasmine.

But Jasmine was looking at the door. "I hear something," she said. Two days earlier the doctor had said that Jasmine's mother was about to give birth. Now whenever Jasmine heard a noise, she was sure the baby was coming.

From downstairs came the sound of a door slamming.

"The baby's coming. I've got to boil water," Jasmine said. She jumped up.

"Wait a second," said May. "Could that be the slamming of an oven door?"

From downstairs came a sweet, buttery smell.

"Could we be smelling fresh-baked cookies?" asked Corey.

Jasmine sat back down. "It is cookies," she said. "Rats."

"It could be worse," May said with a grin. "After all, your mother's cookies are—"

"—the greatest," Corey said.

They went back to playing with their model ponies. A few minutes later there was a knock at the door of Jasmine's room. The door was open, but one of the nice things about Mrs. James was that she never came into Jasmine's room without knocking.

Jasmine Helps a Foal

"Hi, Mom," Jasmine said.

"Hi, Mrs. J.," May said. May had known Mrs. James forever. Actually, she had known Mrs. James before forever because Mrs. James and her mom had been friends when they were pregnant with Jasmine and May.

"Hi, Mrs. J.," Corey said.

Mrs. James walked awkwardly into the room. Normally she was thin and delicate, just like Jasmine. Now that she was pregnant, her stomach was enormous.

Mrs. James put one hand in the small of her back. Her other hand held a tray.

"Are you okay, Mrs. J.?" May asked.

"I'm fine," Mrs. James said. "Except sometimes I have the feeling I'm going to tip over."

She walked to the rug where the girls were sitting and looked down at them with a worried expression.

May knew right away why Mrs. James looked worried. She was trying to figure out how to put the tray down without tipping over.

May hopped up. "If there's anything I'm good at, it's holding trays," she said. "Besides, I'm starving."

Jasmine Helps a Foal

With a grateful smile, Mrs. James handed the tray to her. "Thanks, May," she said. "There's oatmeal cookies and apple juice."

May found that holding the tray was not easy. It took both hands to keep it steady, and even then the glasses wobbled. Being very careful, she lowered the tray to the rug.

"Just the thing for ponies," Corey said. "Oats and apples."

"My mom knows," said Jasmine proudly.

They picked up their model ponies and pretended to let them take a drink of the apple juice. The girls made the ponies sip and snort with pleasure.

"Do you think they'd like cookies?" Jasmine said.

"Anyone would like your mother's cookies," said May.

They let the ponies nibble the cookies.

May couldn't help thinking that it was a good thing model ponies didn't actually eat or drink. She was hungry and thirsty and needed all the cookies and juice she could get.

The three girls leaned against the foot of Jasmine's bed.

"Yummm," they all said at the same time.

They turned to each other, ready to say "Jake" and give high fives, which was what the Pony Tails always did when they said the same thing at the same time. Then they saw that each of them had a cookie in one hand and a glass in the other, so slapping high fives wasn't a great idea. Instead, they grinned and just said, "Jake."

The Pony Tails weren't a club, just best friends. Jasmine James, Corey Takamura, and May Grover rode their ponies together, took classes at Pine Hollow Stables together, and belonged to the same Pony Club. They were even next-door neighbors.

"You don't know how lucky you are," said May.

"Urmf," said Jasmine, her mouth full of cookie.

"You're getting a younger sister—or brother." May took a sip of her apple juice. "Older is very bad. I can't tell you how *totally* bad it is."

"I wonder if I'll be like Dottie and Ellie," Jasmine said. Dottie and Ellie were May's older sisters.

"You'll never be like them," May said. "They're so dumb they don't even like horses."

Jasmine Helps a Foal

The three of them shook their heads. May's father was a horse trainer, and the Grovers always had a stableful of horses, so Dottie and Ellie could have ridden as much as they wanted. But did they want to? No way. Instead, they sat around and talked about boys and soccer. It didn't make sense to May and her friends.

"You're lucky your family is growing," Corey said.

Corey's parents were divorced. Sometimes the new house where Corey and her mom lived felt empty without her father. It helped that Corey got to see her father a lot. It also helped to have the world's nuttiest pets, like Bluebeard the parrot and Dracula the dog. Still, she wished she had a baby brother or sister.

"I've got this baby thing all planned," Jasmine said. "First I'm going to put pictures of ponies around the baby's crib."

"Good thinking," May said.

"And then I'll tell pony stories," said Jasmine.

"The best kind of stories," said Corey.

"And then I'll give the baby a few all-important riding tips. Like to keep her heels down."

Pony Tails

"You can't start keeping your heels down too soon," May agreed.

The three of them enjoyed the crunchy cookies in silence for a moment.

"I heard there's a new foal at Pine Hollow," May said then.

"A new foal!" said Jasmine. She loved foals. "Tell me about it."

"That's all I know," May said. "Maybe Corey knows more."

Corey's mother was a veterinarian. Everybody called her Doc Tock. She didn't work with horses, but she knew everything there was to know about the animals of Willow Creek.

"What's the foal like?" Jasmine asked.

"He's average," said Corey with a shrug. "Nothing special."

An average foal! There was no such thing. Jasmine and May looked at each other in amazement.

"Since when did you think a foal was average?" Jasmine asked.

"This one is," Corey said casually. "Now if you want to see something truly amazing, come to my house and see the baby dachshunds."

Jasmine Helps a Foal

But Jasmine wasn't about to be distracted. "What does the colt look like?" she asked. "What are his markings?"

"Average markings," said Corey. "Now about those dachshunds."

"Is he frisky?" May asked. "Does he like to kick up his heels?"

"*Will somebody let me tell about the dachshunds?*" Corey asked.

May and Jasmine looked at each other and rolled their eyes. Why was Corey acting so strange?

"Okay, tell us about those whatchama-callits," May said grumpily.

"What is a dachshund, anyway?" asked Jasmine.

Corey looked relieved to have their attention at last. "You know those dogs that look like long, furry hot dogs?"

"The ones that are two inches off the ground?" asked Jasmine.

"That's it," Corey said. "Well, the mother hot dog has six little hot dogs."

"Cocktail franks!" said May. When her mother had a party she often served tiny hot dogs.

"They'll be staying at my place for the

next couple of weeks," Corey said. "You have got to see them."

There was a knock on the door. Mr. James poked his head into the room. His blue eyes were twice as big as usual, and his curly hair was a mess. He looked happy and scared at the same time.

"It's . . . ," he said. "I mean . . . now. It's *coming*."

The Pony Tails looked at each other.

"Mom's in labor," Jasmine gasped. "She's going to have the baby."

The three Pony Tails jumped to their feet.

"Zowie!" May said.

2 Keeping Busy

May and Corey stood at the sink rinsing the glasses and the cookie plate from their snack. They put them in the dishwasher and wiped off the tray. Jasmine was at the stove boiling water for the nurse-midwife, who had gotten to the house a few minutes earlier to help her mother.

May didn't want to leave. "We could help you boil water," she said to Jasmine. "What I don't know about boiling water isn't worth knowing."

"That's okay," Jasmine said. "My father and I practiced. I know what to do."

"But we could help you do it even better," May said as she dried her hands and hung up the dishtowel.

"Ahem," Corey said.

May turned to look. Corey was pointing at the back door.

"I could write an article for the school paper," May said. "It would make a great story. 'Mrs. James Gives Birth. Jasmine Gets New Sister.'"

Gently Corey took May's arm and pulled her toward the door.

"It would be on the front page," May said.

Corey pulled May into the mudroom, which was behind the kitchen.

"Gee," said May, "why do I get the feeling that you think it's time to go?"

"Because it *is* time to go," said Corey. "Bye, Jasmine," she called through the doorway.

"See you," said Jasmine.

As May and Corey put on their riding boots, May said, "I still think the Jameses could use our help."

"It's just a wild guess—but I think the nurse-midwife can handle it," Corey said.

Corey opened the back door. A sweet smell hit them. It was a combination of flowers, warm earth, and grass.

"Spring!" May said. "An outstanding time of year. An ideal time to be born."

"Just like you were," Corey said with a

smile. May was called May because she had been born in May.

They headed to the back of Jasmine's yard and onto the Pony Trail. This was a trail that led between the three houses of the Pony Tails.

"Wait until you see the baby dachshunds," Corey said.

They ambled into the Takamuras' barn. In the tack room was a box with very low sides so that the mother dachshund could get in and out. She was lying in the center with a happy look on her face. Around her were six tiny brown babies with their eyes closed. They were making tiny birdlike peeps as they wriggled toward their mother.

"Oh," May said. "I thought dachshunds sounded boring. But these are cute." She leaned over and touched one of the babies' backs. It was silky and warm. "I can't believe they'll ever be big enough to run around the barn."

"Just wait," Corey said. "Babies grow really fast."

May remembered the foal at Pine Hollow. "I can't wait to see that foal," she said.

Corey looked sad. "His mother died."

May sat back on her heels. Suddenly she

didn't feel very cheerful. "I heard she was sick, but I thought she'd get well."

"Everyone did their best," Corey said. "Max was there." Max Regnery was the owner of Pine Hollow Stables. "Judy was there." Judy Barker was the veterinarian who took care of the horses of Willow Creek. "But when the mare was giving birth things went wrong, and there was nothing they could do."

Corey looked so miserable that May put her arms around her. "I guess that's why you didn't want to talk about the foal in front of Jasmine," May said. "You didn't want her to know that sometimes mothers die."

Corey nodded.

"Me and my big mouth," May said. "Sometimes I think I should have an On-Off switch so people can stop me."

"You didn't know," Corey said. "How could you?"

"I bet her owners miss her," May said.

"They were building a special new stable for her and the colt," Corey said. "That's why she was staying at Pine Hollow when she had her baby."

"She'll never see the stable," May said

Jasmine Helps a Foal

sadly. She thought of the empty stall waiting for a horse that would never come.

"The owners can't take care of the colt, so he's going to stay at Pine Hollow," Corey said. "Another mare just foaled, and she has milk enough for two. But she won't let the colt near her. So Max says we'll have to milk the mare and then put the milk in bottles for the colt."

"Hey, I could help," May said, feeling better. At least there was something she could do.

"We all will," Corey said. "Max says the foal is going to need all the help he can get."

A wind blew through the magnolia tree next to the barn, scattering petals toward the ground. The petals had a soft, sweet smell.

From inside the Grovers' barn in the yard next door came a whinny.

"That's Mac," May said, recognizing her own pony's voice. She cocked her head. The whinny came again. "I get the feeling that Macaroni is dying for a ride."

Corey's pony was in the paddock behind the Takamuras' barn. He answered Macaroni's whinny with one of his own.

"I have the feeling Samurai feels the same," Corey said.

"Coming," said May and Corey at the same time. They would have given each other high fives and said "Jake" because they had said the same thing at the same time. But Jasmine wasn't there. So instead Corey and May grinned.

Ten minutes later they met on ponyback at the gate behind Corey's barn. Macaroni, May's pony, was as yellow as macaroni and cheese. Usually Macaroni was easygoing and slow, which was how he got his nickname, Mellow Yellow. But today he looked positively frisky. Samurai, Corey's pony, had a blaze on his face like a samurai sword. Sam danced from one foot to the other.

May opened the gate that led to the field behind the barns. After Sam and Corey had ridden through, May closed the gate. The people who owned the field didn't mind if the Pony Tails rode there as long as they closed the gates.

Samurai snorted and shook his head, ready to take off.

"Walk!" Corey said. She knew the ponies

had to warm up first. Otherwise they might pull a muscle.

Even Macaroni wanted to run.

"I know it's spring," May said. "But we're walking."

First the ponies walked. Then Corey and May let them trot. When Mac and Sam had worked up a light sweat, May and Corey looked at each other and grinned. "I think," Corey said.

"Totally," May said.

Corey tightened her reins.

May leaned slightly forward.

All of a sudden the ponies were cantering alongside each other in a wonderful rocking motion. They cantered along the edge of the field, under a big oak tree, and to the bottom of a hill. Then the girls pulled the ponies into a walk and rode slowly up the hill.

At the top, they stopped their ponies and took in the view. Looking as tiny as a picture in a book were the barns of Pine Hollow Stables. May and Corey could see Red O'Malley, the stable hand, forking hay into a wheelbarrow. They could see Max Regnery riding a horse in the paddock.

Corey and May turned the ponies around

to look back at their own houses. On the left was Jasmine's house, looking as small as a doll's house. Pink tulips bloomed next to the steps. A wreath of forsythia hung on the door. Everything looked pretty and peaceful.

But something mysterious was happening inside.

3 A Long, Lonely Wait

"Don't cry," Jasmine said. "I'll take care of you."

The doll's expression didn't change. She stared at Jasmine with blank blue eyes.

"Everything is going to be fine," Jasmine said.

The doll didn't look upset. In fact, the doll didn't look very much of anything. Jasmine was practicing. Her parents had given her the doll a couple of weeks earlier. They said she could hold it and pretend to feed it.

The doll wasn't very good company. It didn't talk. It didn't know anything about ponies. It just lay there and stared.

Down the hall, Jasmine could hear her parents talking.

Jasmine Helps a Foal

Her father was saying, "Breathe, breathe."

Her mother was making puffing sounds. It reminded Jasmine of a book she used to love called *The Little Engine that Could*. She remembered that in the book the engine had to puff its way up an enormous hill. Jasmine thought it sounded as if her mother was doing the same thing.

Jasmine had gone into her parents' bedroom a couple of times. Her mother looked fine. She was a little sweaty, and her father kept wiping her forehead with a damp washcloth. Her long, curly hair was tangled on the pillow, but she didn't seem to care about her hairdo right then.

The nurse-midwife looked confident and smart, so Jasmine was sure she was doing a good job. Down the hall Jasmine could hear the midwife's low, friendly voice. Then she heard her mother saying something Jasmine couldn't understand.

Jasmine noticed that the doll was staring at her.

"I didn't forget about you," she said to the doll. "I was just listening. You know how it is when something really exciting happens.

You can't help listening." She picked the doll up and held it to her chest. "You're number one with me."

Jasmine liked her model ponies better, so this was not really true. But she didn't want the doll to feel bad.

She crossed her legs Indian style and put the doll in her lap. Her bed was covered with books about babies and baby-sitting. She picked up her favorite, Babysitters Club #102, *Mary Anne and the Little Princess*.

"You're really going to like this," she said to the doll. "The plot is a zinger." Jasmine wriggled until she and the doll were comfortable, and then she started to read out loud.

Before Jasmine knew it, she had read an entire chapter. "I guess you liked that," she said to the doll. "Your concentration is excellent." Jasmine grinned because her teacher was always telling her class that they had the attention span of fleas.

"How about another chapter?" Jasmine asked. The doll seemed to feel that this would be fine. Jasmine's back was tired, so she lay on her side with the doll next to her. She began to read more and more slowly.

She yawned. The words in the book seemed to stretch out forever.

The next thing she knew, something sharp was poking her. She opened her eyes and saw that she was lying on a corner of the book. She had fallen asleep, she realized. She looked at the doll and saw that she was lying on her back, staring at the ceiling.

"I'm really sorry," Jasmine said. "I must have dozed off."

She sat up and pulled the doll into her lap. "You know what I was dreaming about?"

The doll didn't answer.

"I was dreaming about riding," Jasmine said. "I was having this really wild ride. We were galloping down the road."

The doll stared.

"We didn't even warm up," said Jasmine with a grin. "If Max had been in my dream he would have been furious."

There was a knock on her door. It was her father.

"Progress report," he said.

"Is everything okay?" Jasmine said with a sudden stab of worry.

"More than okay," Mr. James said. "Superbly okay. Stunningly okay." One of the things about Jasmine's father was that the more excited he got, the longer his words got.

"She's here!" he said. "The baby." He let out a huge sigh of relief. "The most beautiful baby on earth."

"She?" Jasmine said.

"Your new sister," Mr. James said. "Sophie."

Jasmine leaped to her feet. And then she realized she was standing on the bed. She jumped down and ran over to her father and hugged him. He leaned down to hug her, and she felt something wet on her cheek. She looked up. Her father's eyes were shiny. He was crying because he was so happy.

"Come on," he said, and took her hand.

The hall with its shiny wood floor seemed long. Jasmine and her father tiptoed along it as if someone were asleep.

"Why are we tiptoeing?" Jasmine whispered.

Her father looked surprised. "Um . . ." He grinned. "Good question."

Jasmine giggled, and they both took regular steps the rest of the way.

Jasmine Helps a Foal

Jasmine stopped in the doorway of her parents' bedroom. Her mother was sitting up in bed. Her hair had been brushed, and a pink ribbon was holding it back. Her face was shiny and clean. In her arms was the baby.

At first all Jasmine saw was a white flannel bundle. It was large, bigger than Jasmine had expected. She stepped closer. At one end of the bundle was a tiny, grumpy red face surrounded by messy brown hair.

"Oh," Jasmine said. She thought there must be something wrong with the baby because it was so ugly.

"Isn't she beautiful?" her mother asked.

"Totally," Jasmine said, feeling sorry for her mother. Imagine giving birth to something like that! Jasmine looked up at her father. He was gazing at the baby with pride.

Wait a second, Jasmine thought. If there was something wrong with the baby, her father wouldn't look so proud. Jasmine stepped closer to get a better look. The baby had spiky brown hair that was all different lengths. Among other things, this baby needed a haircut.

Jasmine Helps a Foal

"Say hello to your new sister," Mrs. James said.

"Hello, Sophie," said Jasmine.

Sophie made a sound like a grumpy cat.

Jasmine leaned closer because she knew that newborn babies can't see very far.

"I'm Jasmine, your sister."

Sophie let loose an ear-piercing scream. Jasmine couldn't believe that someone so small could make such a horrible sound.

"I was just trying to be nice," Jasmine said.

"It's probably her diaper," Mrs. James said. "Maybe it needs changing."

"Let me do that," said Mr. James, rushing forward.

Mrs. James gave Mr. James the baby. The nurse-midwife rushed over with a package of baby wipes. Mr. James laid Sophie on the changing table and unwrapped her clothes. First there was the white flannel layer. And then a yellow cotton one. And then another white one. And then Sophie was wearing a cotton T-shirt with an undershirt beneath it. Talk about the layered look, Jasmine thought.

Inside was a tiny body with wiggling arms and legs.

Sophie let out a yell. She waved her fists and kicked her feet. Her face turned purple with rage.

Sophie might be little, Jasmine thought, but she sure knew how to get attention.

4 A Family Welcome

"Not like that," Jasmine said. It was amazing. Her father was an ecologist. He had a doctor's degree in biology, but he still didn't know how to make a proper veggie burger.

"You use both hands," Jasmine said, showing him how to pat the top and bottom of the burger at the same time.

"I'll never get it," he said, looking gloomily at the plate of burgers.

"It takes practice," Jasmine said. "You do the last one." She passed the bowl to him. Carefully he lifted out the gloppy veggie mix.

It was quiet now. The nurse-midwife had gone home, and Mrs. James and Sophie were asleep. The refrigerator was giving off a comfortable hum. Picklepuss, Jasmine's cat, was snoozing on top of it.

Mr. James finished the burger and stepped back to take a look. The burger was lumpy. "It's not as good as yours," he said.

"You did your best," Jasmine said. She carried the burgers over to the stove and sprayed a tiny amount of cooking oil in a nonstick pan. She put the pan on the burner, laid the burgers in the pan, and turned on the flame.

"You really know what to do," her dad said.

"No big deal," she said, going back to the kitchen table to snap the green beans. She pulled out her chair and sat down. "Would you believe there are kids at school who don't like veggie burgers?" she said.

"Inexplicable," Mr. James said. "Incomprehensible." What he meant was that he was surprised.

They settled back in their chairs. So far this day had been pretty exciting. Jasmine was glad to have a moment of peace.

"I like my doll," Jasmine said. "She's really cute."

"It's good to practice," her father said.

Jasmine Helps a Foal

"When you were born I didn't know what I was doing. I was a total ignoramus."

"A what?" Jasmine asked.

"A total dummy," her father said. "When they gave you to me in the hospital, I was afraid I was going to drop you. I held you so awkwardly, you started yowling." He smiled. "I was afraid they were going to fire me as a father."

"They don't fire fathers," she said.

"You never know," he said with a grin. One of the nice things about her father was that he had a great sense of humor.

"It's so much better this way," he said. "In the hospital I didn't know how to behave. I felt like I couldn't do anything right."

"It's like gymnastics class!" said Jasmine. "I'm always sure I'm about to fall on my head."

Her father nodded sympathetically. "You're so worried about whether you're doing the right thing, you do the wrong thing."

"You should see me turn cartwheels," Jasmine said. "It's pathetic."

She began to relax.

"Sophie is cool," she said.

Her father nodded.

"I was kind of worried about having a new baby in the house," Jasmine said.

"But now you see how great she is," her father said.

From upstairs came a high-pitched wail, like a frightened cat. Then it changed to a deeper note, like an enraged cow. Sophie might not be able to do much, Jasmine thought, but she'd learned how to scream.

Mr. James jumped to his feet. "She'll wake Mom." He ran out of the room. Then Jasmine could hear him taking the stairs two at a time.

The veggie burgers were sizzling. Jasmine went to look at them. She could tell from the crisp, toasty smell that the first side was done. She got the spatula and turned the burgers over. She checked to see if the water for the beans was boiling. When she saw that it was, she dropped the beans into the pot. She set the table for two. Then she waited for the food to cook. She thought about her family, which was growing, and Corey's family, which was shrinking. One thing about families, she thought—they're always changing.

When the food was cooked, Jasmine arranged a platter with the burgers in the middle and the green beans in a ring outside. It looked almost like a restaurant dish, she thought proudly. She waited and waited. Sophie wasn't crying anymore. Jasmine wondered what had happened to her father.

There is nothing worse than a lukewarm veggie burger, she thought. She decided she had to do something.

She climbed the stairs.

Her father was sitting in the rocker next to the bed. He must have changed Sophie and given her to Jasmine's mother. Mrs. James was nursing Sophie.

Sophie wasn't an angry bright pink anymore. She was a beautiful, healthy shade of white that had a little bit of pink in it.

"I bet Petalpuss is going to have a big burp after this," Mr. James said with a happy smile.

"I think so," said Mrs. James. Gently she smoothed Sophie's hair.

"What did you call me when I was just born?" Jasmine asked Mr. James.

He looked up with a grin. "Petalpuss. Because your face was like a flower."

That's great, Jasmine thought. He took my

nickname and gave it to Sophie without even asking.

She stood up. "I guess I'd better eat my veggie burger," she said. "There's nothing worse than a cold veggie burger." This was a hint. She was hoping her father would come and eat his burger.

"I'll be down in a minute," he said. But Jasmine could tell from the sound of his voice that it would be a very long minute.

When she got downstairs, she served herself a burger and a heap of green beans. She took a bite of the burger, but it tasted bland. She went to the refrigerator and got a bottle of ketchup. She slathered the burger with it. Then the burger had a sour ketchupy taste.

She sat there poking at the pieces of her burger, wondering why she was stuck down here when everybody else was upstairs. How come her father hadn't asked her to bring the veggie burgers upstairs so they could all eat together?

Jasmine knew the answer. Her parents didn't care. They had forgotten about her.

Picklepuss, the cat, stretched, stood up, and jumped off the top of the refrigerator.

Jasmine Helps a Foal

Without making a sound, the cat headed out the kitchen door and up the stairs.

Great, Jasmine thought, she'd rather be with the new baby, too.

Jasmine got up and scraped her plate into the garbage. She rinsed the plate and put it in the dishwasher. She rinsed her glass and put it in, too. They looked pretty lonely there. Jasmine wondered if it was going to be like this all the time—one lonely meal after another.

Then she had a wonderful thought. The Pony Tails would understand. All she had to do was call them.

Jasmine stepped over to the phone, which hung on the wall next to the refrigerator. She picked it up. But instead of a dial tone, she heard her father's voice. He was talking to Jasmine's grandmother.

"She's the greatest baby in the world," Mr. James was saying excitedly. "She's beautiful. She's brilliant."

"Hi, Grandma," Jasmine said.

"Jasmine," her grandmother said. "You must be tickled pink to have a new baby in the house."

Jasmine wondered what her grandma

meant by tickled pink. She figured her grandma meant pleased.

"It's nice," Jasmine said. "She's cute. You know what, Grandma? There's a new foal at Pine Hollow."

"It's that time of year," her grandma said cheerfully. "Now tell me everything about Sophie."

Jasmine realized that her grandma was talking to her father, not to her.

"She has the bluest eyes," Mr. James said. "And she has the curliest hair."

"I can't wait to see her," Jasmine's grandma said. "I'm going to give her the world's biggest kiss."

5 A Newborn in Trouble

Golden light slanted through the fence, and the air was filled with the sweet perfume of budding flowers.

"I can see why animals like to be born in spring," said May. "It's a great time of year."

In a paddock at Pine Hollow horses were munching grass and frisking in the warm spring air.

"When I left home, Mom and Sophie were snoozing next to an open window," Jasmine said. "They looked really happy."

"Sounds good," said May.

"It wasn't like that when I was born," Jasmine said gloomily.

Corey and May turned to look at her with surprise.

"How do you know how things were when you were born?" May asked. "Do you remember?"

"My father told me," Jasmine said. "He says it was a real nightmare."

"How could it be a nightmare? It was your birth," Corey said. "Your parents must have been happy."

"My father thought he was going to be fired as a father," Jasmine said. "It was that bad."

Corey and May exchanged looks. Jasmine sounded pretty down.

"Horse Wise, come to order," said Max Regnery. Horse Wise was Pine Hollow's Pony Club. All the serious younger riders at Pine Hollow belonged to Horse Wise.

"I have two announcements to make," said Max, his blue eyes twinkling. "First, I want to announce that Jasmine James has a new sister. Her name is Sophie." He pulled a piece of paper from his pocket. "At birth she weighed about seven and a half pounds."

The riders looked puzzled because usually babies came in exact pounds and ounces.

Max raised his hand. "I know you're

Jasmine Helps a Foal

wondering why she's *about* seven and a half pounds. It's because she was born at home. To weigh her, Mr. James got on the bathroom scales to see how much he weighed. Then he got on again with Sophie in his arms. He subtracted the first weight from the second weight and got Sophie's weight." When the riders looked puzzled, Max explained, "The weight of Mr. James holding Sophie, minus Mr. Jame's weight, gives Sophie's weight."

"Hey, it's like a math problem," said May.

The members of Horse Wise cheered. They turned to Jasmine to applaud her not just for having a new sister, but for having such a smart father.

Jasmine grinned. She was tired from getting woken up twice the night before by Sophie's crying, but hearing everyone cheer for Sophie made her feel better.

"And now for the other baby," Max said.

A ripple of anxiety ran through Horse Wise. Everybody knew about the colt. Everybody knew the colt was an orphan.

"The colt was born last Sunday," Max said. "Judy Barker did everything she could to save the mother, but it wasn't possible."

A gloomy silence descended over Horse Wise. There was nothing worse than the death of a horse, especially a mother horse.

"A mare gives more than milk to her foal," Max said. "She also provides love and security."

The riders nodded.

"A mare makes her foal feel safe."

Jasmine thought of the white picket fence around her family's house, the tulips blooming beside the back door, and the mudroom with its orderly rows of boots and shoes. That was what her parents did, she realized. They made things safe.

"How can he feel safe if he doesn't have a mother?" May asked.

"Good question," said Max. "It's difficult, but not impossible. If all of you help, we can give this colt a good beginning. Come with me. I want you to see him."

Max led them to the foaling box, which was a large stall that had been layered with clean straw that was built up on the sides to keep out drafts.

The colt got to his feet, wobbling on his long legs.

He had big, soft eyes that cried out for

Jasmine Helps a Foal

love. And long ears. Those were ears a mother should lick. He had a little stubble on his chin. And his nose was running a tiny bit. Max pulled a tissue from his pocket and gently wiped the colt's nose.

The colt put his nose next to Max's arm and nudged it, as if he were looking for something.

"He misses his mother," Max said.

A sigh went up from the riders.

"Can I hug him?" said one of the younger riders.

"You can later. This colt is going to need lots of hugs," Max said. "But right now he wants to eat."

The colt turned from Max to Jasmine, who was standing next to him. The colt put his nose next to Jasmine's face and nuzzled her. She could feel his scratchy whiskers and his warm, steamy breath. She put her arms around his neck and hugged him. His heart was beating fast. He was nervous. She brushed the forelock out of his eyes. His eyes locked onto hers. She felt as if he was saying "I'm scared. Help me."

"I'm going to show you how to feed him," Max said. He led them into the tack room,

where there was a big white box. "This is a bottle warmer," he said. "An hour ago we milked the mare that already had a baby. We put the bottle of milk in here so it will be warm for the colt." Max lifted the bottle and shook it, sending a couple of drops onto his left wrist. "It's just the right temperature," he said. "The milk should never be too cold or too hot."

Max walked out of the tack room into the stable with all of Horse Wise following him. When he got to the foaling box, he opened the door. The colt was standing there, his nose up, his eyes bright.

Max held the bottle a few inches above the colt's nose. The colt stuck out his lips, grasped the nipple, and started sucking hard, making loud slurping sounds.

The milk in the bottle disappeared slowly.

"You don't want him to nurse too fast or he'll get air in his stomach. That's why the hole in the nipple is small," Max said. He turned to the members of Horse Wise. "Who wants to hold the bottle?"

Almost every hand went up.

"You have to hold tight, or he'll suck the bottle right out of your hand," Max said.

Corey went first. Max wasn't kidding. The colt was strong. She had to hold on to the bottle with both hands. But it was fun.

May was next. The colt was nursing so hard that the bottle jiggled, which made her hands itch. "It tickles," she said.

Almost every member of Horse Wise had a turn. Finally only a few riders hadn't held the bottle. One of them was Jasmine.

"Go ahead," Corey said to her. "You'll love it."

"That's okay," Jasmine said. She could tell everyone else loved feeding the colt, but she just didn't feel like it.

May had opened her mouth, about to urge Jasmine to try it, when Corey shook her head.

When the bottle was empty, Max led them to a spot under the big magnolia tree where Horse Wise liked to meet. May lay back on the grass. The magnolia flowers were beginning to lose their petals. One white petal fell lazily onto her arm.

"There's a reason I had you feed the colt," Max said. "He has to learn to be comfortable with a variety of strangers because he has to be fed every two hours. Who wants to sign up?"

Jasmine Helps a Foal

Hands shot up.

"First you have to check with your parents to see which feeding times are all right," Max said. He passed out permission slips for parents to sign.

"I may move to Pine Hollow for a while," said May as she slipped the paper into her pocket.

"I'll get my mother to give me special bottle-feeding tips," Corey said.

They turned to Jasmine, expecting her to say that she couldn't wait to feed the foal. But Jasmine turned away.

Corey and May looked at each other and shrugged. Maybe Jasmine was tired of babies.

6 "It Figures!"

The girls piled out of the Grovers' station wagon in front of May's house.

"I've got to ride," May said. "I'll die if I don't."

Unmounted meetings of Horse Wise were interesting, but they were also frustrating. May felt as if she needed to ride for a week.

"Me too," Corey said. She looked at the sun. It was still high in the sky. "We've got time," she said. "I'll bring Samurai over."

They turned to Jasmine. "I could use a ride," she said. Jasmine didn't actually feel much like riding, but she wanted to be with Corey and May.

Jasmine walked through the back door of

her house, through the mudroom, and into the kitchen. On the kitchen table was a stack of baby clothes. It was amazing how many outfits Sophie had for someone who'd been around for less than a day, Jasmine thought. On the refrigerator door was Sophie's birth certificate. A week earlier, Jasmine's drawing of Outlaw had been there, but now it was gone. It figures, Jasmine thought.

Jasmine poked her head into her parents' room because she wanted to tell them about the new colt. Her mother was sound asleep, her mouth open. Sophie was snoozing in the crib.

Jasmine went to look for her father. He was pecking away at his computer.

"What do you think of Times New Roman?" he said.

"What?" Jasmine said.

"It's the typeface for the birth announcement," he said. His forehead creased with anxiety. "Maybe Times New Roman is too formal. Maybe Bodoni is better. What do you think?"

"There's a new colt at Pine Hollow," Jasmine said.

"Great," her father said. "Take a look at

this and give me your honest opinion." He passed her a birth announcement that said:

Announcing
the birth of
Sophia Maria Rogers James

"What's Maria Rogers?" Jasmine asked.

"Those are her middle names," her father explained.

"Do I have middle names?" Jasmine asked.

"Of course you have a middle name," her father said. "It's Alice."

Alice! Some great middle name. "It figures," Jasmine said. She walked away. As she left the room she heard her father pecking at the computer.

Jasmine went into her room. She changed into blue jeans and a T-shirt. Since she knew it might get cold, she decided to put on a jacket. Her new blue-jean jacket would be just right. She went to the hall closet to get it.

The closet was stuffed with boxes of diapers.

Figures, Jasmine thought. She went back

Jasmine Helps a Foal

into her room and dug an old sweatshirt out of the closet. The sleeves were a little short, but what else could she do?

She went out to the barn. The minute she opened the door she heard Outlaw nicker.

"Hey, pal," she said to him.

He nickered more loudly. As she entered his stall, he bobbed his head, the white mask shape on his face gleaming.

She put her arms around him and buried her face in his soft coat. All of a sudden she felt as if she was going to cry. This is silly, she thought. She remembered that Deborah, Max's wife, once said that when you feel like crying you should take five deep breaths. Jasmine took one, two, three. She was beginning to feel better.

Outlaw nuzzled her ear.

"You understand," she said, turning toward him. But when she looked at Outlaw she saw that he had bright, eager eyes. He was dying to go out. He wasn't offering sympathy. He was telling her to get moving.

"It figures," she said.

But Outlaw was right. There was no point in moping around the barn. She got the carrier full of grooming equipment and gave

Outlaw a brushing. Then she tacked him up and led him outside.

May was sitting on Macaroni. Corey was on Sam.

"I was thinking today would be a good day for a TT," said May.

TT stood for total training. On some days the girls liked to put the ponies through their paces. The girls loved it, and the ponies loved it, too.

"Samurai's canter has been ragged lately," Corey said. "I mean really ragged. I don't know what to do."

"Hey, you know what Max says," May said. "When you have a problem, take a deep breath and think."

"This may need two deep breaths," Corey said.

"Macaroni's halt after a trot is a real problem," May said. "I guess we'll work on that."

May and Corey looked at Jasmine, waiting for her to say what she wanted to work on. But Jasmine didn't feel like a TT.

She didn't want to hurt May's and Corey's feelings, so she said, "I'd better get home. I told my parents I wouldn't stay long."

"But you just came," May said. "Think of Outlaw."

"Ahem," Corey said.

May stopped talking.

"I guess you have a lot of work with the baby," Corey said.

"Sure," Jasmine said. "Loads of things." She didn't want to admit that at home there was absolutely nothing for her to do.

Jasmine turned Outlaw toward the barn. He started walking and then stopped and looked at the wide field behind the barn. His brown eyes were wide. He seemed to be saying "Let's go!"

"Sorry," Jasmine said to him. "I have to help Mom and Dad." Then she had a funny thought: I'm lying to my pony. Is that dumb or what? She sighed and rubbed Outlaw's neck. "If you want to know the truth, Outlaw, I'm in a crummy mood."

Jasmine put Outlaw in his stall. She gave him fresh hay and water and headed for the house.

In the mudroom she sat down to pull off her boots. From upstairs came the sound of Sophie crying.

Great, Jasmine thought. Here we go

again. It's like a TV show you can't turn off.

Sophie cried more loudly.

Jasmine looked at her boots. She decided not to take them off. She got up and walked out the back door, being careful to not let it slam.

She went to the barn and put her arms around Outlaw.

"You deserve a ride," she said to him.

Outlaw nickered and nodded.

She got his saddle and bridle and tacked him up again. She led him out of the barn and mounted him.

Outlaw headed toward the ring behind May's house, assuming that they were going to join Macaroni and Samurai.

As they got close to the ring, Jasmine raised her hand. But May and Corey didn't see her. May was telling Corey something. It was as if Jasmine weren't there. They had forgotten about her completely. It figured.

"Let's go for a long, long ride," Jasmine said to Outlaw. "Let's ride forever."

7 A Visit to Pine Hollow

Suddenly Jasmine realized that she was alone in the middle of the field. Everything else was far away—houses, trees, Willow Creek, the highway. She felt like the only person on earth.

She stopped Outlaw and looked up. A hawk was circling in the sky, making tiny cries. Jasmine looked down and saw the wind ripple through the grass.

Jasmine pressed her knees against Outlaw's sides, and he began to trot again. His steps were long, his head was high. She felt as if the two of them were floating.

They came to a clump of oak trees and rode through them. As they came out on the other side, Jasmine saw Pine Hollow Stables spread out down below. She saw the white U of the barn, the ring, the paddocks, and the tidy house. She heard a clank and a cough. Red O'Malley's old green car pulled out of the driveway and headed away.

She rode Outlaw down the hill to the front of the barn. Everything was quiet. There were no riders or stable hands around.

She looked over at the house. Max's station wagon wasn't in the driveway. Jasmine remembered that Max had said he and Deborah and his mother were going to a party that afternoon.

The wind rustled the flowers in the magnolia tree. Suddenly Pine Hollow seemed like a lonely place.

Jasmine got down and hugged Outlaw's neck. She looked into his soft brown eyes.

"This is no big deal," she said. "We're not really alone. There are horses, and ponies, and cats, and mice."

She took a deep breath to calm herself. The silence was spooking her, and she didn't want Outlaw to get spooked, too.

"I'm going to say hi to the horses in the barn," she said.

She wanted to make sure that Outlaw was

securely tied, so she hooked a lead rope to his halter, which was under his bridle. Then she tied the rope to the fence.

"I'll be right back," she said, giving Outlaw a pat.

The barn door was shut, so Jasmine went around the side, looking for a way in.

She saw an open window in the feed room. It wasn't very big, but she figured she could squeeze through it. A wheelbarrow stood next to the feed room door. She rolled it under the window and climbed into it. The wheelbarrow rocked. She put her arms out to steady herself. She grabbed the bottom of the open window and pushed it up higher.

She looked at the window and jumped for it. She was half in, half out of the window. She wriggled, waved her feet, and fell forward onto a bale of hay.

She sneezed and rolled over.

A black shadow loomed. Jasmine jumped up and plastered herself against the wall. The shadow was cast by a large bag of carrots on the feed room counter.

"You scared me," she said to the carrots. She laughed at herself for talking to vegetables. That made her feel better.

Jasmine Helps a Foal

She turned and entered the barn. A wonderful warm, soft, steamy smell greeted her. It was the smell of horses. She stopped at the first stall.

"Nickel," she said.

He blinked at her sleepily. He was having his late afternoon nap. Nickel loved naps.

"It's *great* to see you," she said.

Nickel yawned.

She walked to the next stall. "Barq," she said. "I haven't seen you in ages."

Barq shifted from one foot to the other and switched his tail.

"Starlight!" she said. Starlight was one of her favorite horses. Starlight's nose must have itched, because he drew back his lips and snorted.

From the other end of the barn came a high-pitched cry. Jasmine stopped. It came again. It was a high, clear sound like a baby's cry. The hair on the back of Jasmine's neck prickled.

The cry came louder now. It sounded helpless.

It reminded Jasmine of Sophie's cry. She ran toward the sound. It was coming from the foaling box. Jasmine looked over the wall of the box. The long-legged colt was cast. He had lain down so close to the wall that when he tried to get up there wasn't enough room for him to roll and get his legs under him. He was trapped.

His big eyes were full of fear. He was waiting for his mother to come and save him, but he had no mother. There was only one person who could help him.

Jasmine opened the door of the foaling box and stepped inside.

The helpless colt looked up at her with his sad brown eyes. Her heart broke at the sight of such helplessness.

"You'll be okay," she said, and squatted next to him.

His head drooped as if he had given up hope. Jasmine remembered that Max said mothers don't just feed their children. They make them feel safe. Somehow she had to make the colt feel safe.

She tickled his ears. "I'm here," she said. She smoothed his forelock. "Everything will be fine."

His eyes searched hers as if he wanted to believe her.

She kissed him on the end of his velvety-soft nose.

He sighed. He blinked. He put his nose on her knee.

He trusts me, Jasmine thought.

"Put your trust in me," she said, sounding more confident than she felt.

She pulled two of his legs.

Nothing happened. The colt was too heavy for her to move.

She could feel his legs trembling. She put her arms around him and said, "Don't worry." But she could feel his heart beating faster and faster.

Max always said that when you were in a spot, you should take a deep breath and think. She took a deep breath. That part worked, but no ideas came. She saw a shudder run down the colt's long, delicate legs. If only he could get them under him.

8 Jasmine's Rescue Mission

Maybe if she pulled him by all four legs it would help. Carefully Jasmine gathered the colt's four hooves and tugged at them. He didn't move. The colt looked at her with hurt eyes, as if to ask what she was doing.

"I'm sorry," she said. "I guess that wasn't a good idea." She took another deep breath.

From outside the barn came a whinny. Outlaw was tired of waiting. She didn't blame him. She shouldn't have left him there for so long. What if he broke free and escaped? Jasmine was pretty sure she'd tied him securely, but what if she hadn't? In her mind she went over what she'd done. She had clipped the rope to his halter and then tied it tightly to the fence.

Tied. Rope. Suddenly Jasmine had an idea.

"You aren't going to like this, but it's our only hope," she said to the colt.

She stood up. She hated to leave him, but she knew she had to do it. She ran down the barn to the tack room, where she found a piece of rope.

When she got back to the box, she showed the rope to the colt. She let him look at it and then sniff it. He nibbled at it curiously.

"I have to do this," she said.

She made a loop, like a lasso—Max had shown them how to do it at a Horse Wise meeting. She slipped it around the colt's two front legs, and then swiftly around his back legs. Gently she pulled the loop closed, so that his four feet were together.

The colt looked at her with startled eyes.

Jasmine closed her eyes and pulled gently on the rope. There was a tiny movement, nothing more. Jasmine pulled with all her might.

The colt slid toward her. Two, three, four, five inches. That would be enough, she was sure. She untied the knot and released his feet.

Jasmine Helps a Foal

The colt looked at her with his giant eyes. "You can do it," she said. "You can stand." He just lay there, looking at her.

Jasmine remembered seeing a mother horse nudge her colt to get him to stand up. Jasmine bent over and nuzzled the colt's forehead with her nose. His eyelids fluttered. He let out a tiny sigh. She could feel his breath on her face. He pulled his front legs under him, and then his back legs. Wobbling and swaying, he tried to rise on his back legs. Jasmine remembered that the mother horse hadn't helped. She had stood back and let the colt do it himself.

"You're almost there," Jasmine said. "You can do it."

The colt's back legs straightened. His rear was up, but his head was still down on the ground.

"Now for the other half," Jasmine said. "Push."

The colt looked at her, his eyes filled with worry.

"Just do it," Jasmine said.

He closed his eyes. He almost gave up. Then he pushed. His front legs straightened. He was standing!

"Good work," Jasmine said. "I knew you

could do it." She put her arms around his neck and felt his heart beating more slowly now. He wasn't afraid anymore.

"You're strong. You're brave," she whispered in his ear. "You've got what it takes."

As she stood back, the colt shook himself as if to say "Of course I'm strong and brave. What did you think?"

"Hey, I bet you're hungry," she said to the colt. "After all that work, you could use some food."

She walked to the tack room and opened the bottle warmer. Inside was a bottle. Jasmine picked it up and shook a few drops on the back of her hand. The milk was just the right temperature.

She took the bottle back to the foaling box and let herself in. The colt dived for the bottle. He drank so hard, he almost trembled. Jasmine realized that for a colt that was just a few days old, being hungry seemed like the world's biggest crisis.

When he was finished, he had a rim of milk on his lips. He sighed, looking totally satisfied. Jasmine put her arms around him, and he yawned into her hair.

"I didn't want to give you a bottle this

morning because I was tired of babies. They always get all the attention," she said. "But feeding you was fun. And you *need* lots of attention, don't you?"

The colt looked down at the hay that was piled around his stall. And then he looked at Jasmine. She thought maybe he wanted to lie down but he was afraid he wouldn't be able to get up again.

"It's okay," she said to him. She sat down on the stall floor to show him that it was safe.

He folded his long, spindly legs and dropped down next to her.

"You need a rest," said Jasmine, wrapping her arms around his neck again. "I want you to relax." He put his nose in her lap, and within seconds he fell fast asleep.

Jasmine put her head on his neck. "It's been a tough day," she said to the colt, even though he was asleep and couldn't hear her. "But we did okay." Burying her nose in the colt's mane, she fell asleep herself.

When she woke up, it was almost dark. The sky in the window over the foaling stall was dark blue. Jasmine's stomach was rumbling. She was hungry. It was dinnertime.

Outlaw was tied up outside, she remembered. Gently she moved away from the colt. She knew that someone would be coming to feed him soon, so he would be okay. She stood up.

The colt nickered in his sleep and moved his long legs.

"I'll be seeing you," she whispered.

Jasmine ran down the barn aisle, back to the feed room. The window looked really high, but Jasmine knew that if she'd gotten in, she could get out. She stood on the hay bale under the window and jumped. She was halfway through the window when she heard Outlaw whinny again.

"I'm coming," she called. She gave a push and fell out the window.

9 Jasmine Comes Home

Outlaw was grumpy. He glared at Jasmine.

"I had to help the colt," she said.

Outlaw snorted.

"If it had been you, you'd have done the same thing," Jasmine said. "Besides, I fell asleep." She tickled Outlaw in his favorite spot, which was right behind his ears.

"So let's go home," she said.

Outlaw snorted, as if to ask what she was waiting for. She climbed into the saddle, and they headed home.

When they got to the top of the hill, she saw her house. It was tidy and brightly lit. She wanted to be there more than anything. So did Outlaw. He was hungry and tired, she realized. He was longing for his stall.

"We'll be there soon," she said. "I'll give you an extra grooming. You've been a great pony today." Outlaw nodded as if he agreed.

As they walked down the hill Jasmine saw that someone was leaning against the fence behind the barn. It was someone tall and skinny, someone with curly hair. It was her father.

Somehow she had the feeling that he wasn't happy.

Outlaw's steps seemed to get faster and faster.

"No need to rush," Jasmine said to Outlaw. "Take your time."

Jasmine's father climbed the fence and walked toward her.

When he came up to her, his eyes were blazing. "Where have you been?"

Jasmine opened her mouth, about to explain that she had been helping the foal. Before she could say anything, her father spoke up.

"I've been driving all over the neighborhood looking for you," he said. "I was worried sick. Your mother is worried."

"I'm sorry," Jasmine said in a tiny voice.

"I had to get away. Sophie was screaming all the time." She hadn't meant to say anything about Sophie. But now she couldn't stop. "I know she's the greatest human being on earth, but she gets on my nerves."

Jasmine's father reached up and helped Jasmine out of the saddle. On the way down he gave her a hard hug. "You want to know the honest truth? She gets on my nerves sometimes, too." He took Jasmine's hand as she led Outlaw toward the barn. "Anyway, she's not the greatest baby ever born. She's one of the *two* greatest babies ever born. You are the other."

As they walked toward the barn, Jasmine looked at the house. She saw her mother's worried face peering from a window on the second floor. When Mrs. James spotted Jasmine, she waved. "We'll be right in, honey," Mr. James called.

They took Outlaw into the barn and untacked him. Then Jasmine got the carrier full of grooming gear, and she brushed one side of Outlaw while her father brushed the other.

Over Outlaw's back Mr. James said, "I remember when Harry was born." Harry was

Jasmine's uncle. "I kept telling my parents they should take him back to the hospital because he was so ugly."

"No kidding," Jasmine said. She wasn't about to admit that she had thought Sophie was ugly, but this was interesting news.

"All he did was scream," Mr. James said. "I had to stick my fingers in my ears."

"Gee, that's terrible," Jasmine said.

Together she and her father got fresh oats and water for Outlaw. "Harry improved with age," Mr. James said. "He's not half bad now."

Uncle Harry was Jasmine's favorite uncle. It was hard to imagine him as a red-faced, screaming monster. But, if her father said he had been, Jasmine believed him.

As Jasmine and her father walked toward the house, he said, "I guess everything seems different to you now that Sophie's born."

Jasmine was about to say that she hated having one less middle name than Sophie, she hated the way her father had taken her nickname, Petalpuss, and given it to Sophie, and she hated the way her drawing of Outlaw had disappeared from the refrigerator.

Jasmine Helps a Foal

But suddenly she didn't feel so angry anymore.

"Hey," she said. "I can cope."

They walked into the mudroom. Her father waited while she pulled off her riding boots and put on her sneakers. They walked into the kitchen.

Her drawing of Outlaw was hanging in a frame on the wall.

"Wow," she said.

"Do you like the frame?" her father said. "I couldn't decide between black and gold. Gold is more festive, but black is more modern."

Jasmine put her arms around him. "Dad, gold is fine."

They had a long hug.

With her face against her father's chest, Jasmine said, "Was my birth really awful?"

Her father hugged her tight. "It was the greatest day of my life."

"You said it was a nightmare," she said softly.

"The hospital was a nightmare. Not you."

Jasmine looked up at him. Her father's blue eyes were shining.

Jasmine's stomach growled. "Sorry," she said.

"My sentiments exactly," her father said. He picked up a pair of potholders. "As it happens, I have made your favorite meal." He opened the oven. "Vegetable lasagna."

Inside the oven the lasagna was bubbly and brown.

"We're dining upstairs tonight," he said.

Jasmine helped her father load a tray with plates, silverware, and napkins. He went first, carrying the lasagna. She followed him.

It made her think of the night before, when she had to eat her veggie burger alone. As if her father knew what she was thinking, he said, "Sometimes when something exciting happens people get discombobulated." He grinned at his own big word. "I mean they get all mixed up." He looked at her. "I'm sorry."

"What's to be sorry for?" Jasmine said. "You are the world's greatest dad."

Her mother was sitting up in bed.

"Jasmine," she said, reaching out. "Sweetie."

Jasmine dived into her arms. As soon as

Jasmine Helps a Foal

the two of them were hugging, Jasmine re-membered the softness of the bed, and how she and her Mom and Dad loved to watch TV and eat vegetarian pizza together.

Jasmine looked around. Sophie was in her crib looking small and pink—and quiet. When Sophie wasn't screaming, she wasn't half bad.

"Where were you?" her mother said.

"At Pine Hollow. I gave the orphan colt a bottle," Jasmine said.

"Oh," Mrs. James said. "That poor thing. Is he all right now?"

"He's fine," Jasmine said.

"You gave him a bottle?" asked Mrs. James.

Jasmine nodded.

"You know," Mrs. James said, "I was go-ing to give Sophie a bottle of sugar water. But since you know how to feed babies, maybe you could do it."

"You think?" said Jasmine.

"I know you can do it," her mother said.

She went to look into the crib. Sophie was making tiny cheeping noises.

"Where should I feed her?" Jasmine asked.

"Why don't you sit here next to me," her mother said, making room on the bed. She plumped up a pillow for Jasmine to lean on.

As Jasmine settled into the bed, her mother said, "Is that comfortable?"

"Just right," Jasmine said.

Her father picked up Sophie and put her on the changing table to check her diaper. Sophie needed a change, so Mr. James put on a fresh diaper. Then he brought her over to Jasmine.

Sophie looked so small, so fragile, so helpless. What if I drop her? Jasmine thought. What if I feed her wrong? What if she develops the world's biggest burp? But then Jasmine remembered how well she had fed the colt.

Sophie's blue eyes looked up at her. Jasmine slid one hand underneath Sophie's back and another one under her head.

Sophie looked at her with total trust. "It'll be okay," Jasmine whispered to her. "We're sisters." She lifted Sophie, feeling how warm her skin was. She put Sophie against her chest and felt Sophie's tiny hands touch her.

She could feel the beating of Sophie's

heart, and she could tell that Sophie trusted her. Jasmine kissed her on the top of her head.

Jasmine settled Sophie into the crook of her arm. Sophie looked warm and happy, but Jasmine knew she needed to drink.

"Here," Jasmine said, putting the nipple of the bottle next to Sophie's lips.

Sophie sucked it in.

"That was fast," Jasmine said.

As if they were one person, Jasmine and her parents smiled.

Sophie drank an ounce of sugar water, and then she moved her head away from the bottle and looked up at Jasmine.

"Was that good?" Jasmine asked.

Sophie raised her feet with pleasure. Jasmine touched one of them. It was small, but it was strong.

"She has good feet," Jasmine said. "She won't have any problem keeping her heels down as soon as she starts riding." She looked up at her parents. "We'll have to get her a pony someday."

"Absolutely," her father said.

"You'll help us choose it because you know ponies," Mrs. James said.

Jasmine Helps a Foal

One of Sophie's tiny pink hands reached up and touched Jasmine's hand. Sophie's tiny hand closed around one of Jasmine's fingers.

Jasmine bent down and kissed Sophie's tiny thumb.

10 How to Be a Big Sister

"One more thing," May said.

"That's your fifteenth one more thing," Jasmine groaned.

May was filling her in on how *not* to be an older sister.

"Never tell your sister that she's ideal for the Before in a Before and After ad," said May.

"No way," Jasmine said.

"Never lie around and sigh over some pimply TV star," May said.

"I would never do that," Jasmine said.

"Never call boys and hang up," May said.

"As if I would do that," Jasmine said.

"Never paint your toenails green."

"Yuck," Jasmine said.

Jasmine Helps a Foal

"Anyway, you'll never be like my sisters," May said. "You're a normal human being."

"Jasmine's not a normal human being," Corey said. May and Jasmine turned to look at her. "She's a hero."

" 'Did I ever tell you you're my hero?' " May sang.

"Oh, please," Jasmine said. "Give me a break."

"But you are," Corey said. "Max says you really helped the colt. Who knows? Maybe the owners will name him after you."

"A colt named Jasmine?" said May. The three girls giggled.

"I can't believe Max isn't mad at you for climbing in the stable window," Corey said.

"He is," Jasmine said. "I'm going to have to stay late on Friday to polish the tack. I've got stable detention."

"I'll stay, too," Corey said.

"Me too," May said. She sighed. "It's so nice when someone else is in trouble." She turned hastily to Jasmine. "I didn't mean it like that."

"It's okay," Jasmine said with a grin. "Everybody gets in trouble sometimes."

Then a funny thought occurred to Jas-

mine. Someday—when Sophie was bigger—she would get in trouble, too. Not that Jasmine wanted Sophie to be bad or anything. Not that she wanted Sophie to get detention. No way! But in the future, if Sophie did get in trouble, Jasmine would be there to help her little sister out.

It was fun to think of the adventures ahead.

JASMINE'S TIPS
ON HOW A HORSE GROWS

When I look at my tiny little newborn sister, it's hard to imagine that one day she'll be as big as I am. One day she'll even be as old as I am now. Of course, I'll always be her big sister. Right now I'm not worried about that. She's very small; she's got a *lot* of catching up to do.

I don't know whether my sister will ever be bigger than I am, but it's a sure bet that the foal will be—and it won't take all that long, either. Baby horses seem to do a lot of things very quickly. The foal was walking within a half hour after he was born. Sophie

Jasmine's Tips

won't do that for another year! The foal will reach his full height by about the time he's three years old. It will take him longer to fill out. Sophie won't be done with her growing until she's a teenager. The foal is just a few weeks old, and already he's nibbling at grass and hay. Sophie won't get any solid food for months, and when she does, she's going to have to start out with squishy rice cereal and then, if she's lucky, some strained fruit. I think I'd rather eat grass.

I'll always be able to tell how old Sophie is by the number of candles on her cake, but you can't ask a horse how old he is, so there's another way. You look in his mouth and check his teeth. A horse's teeth change as he gets older, and the pattern in each horse is pretty much the same. The teeth won't tell you *exactly* when he's old enough to start school, get a driver's license, or run for president, but it will give you a pretty good idea of how old he is.

Like people, horses get two sets of teeth in their life. The baby teeth are sometimes called milk teeth, because they're the teeth he's got when he's nursing. A foal is born with teeth—usually four on the top and four on the bottom to start with. Sophie has no teeth at all. Mom says she'll start getting teeth when she's about eight months old.

When a foal is a year old, he's got twelve milk teeth, six on top and six on the bottom. They're new and don't show any wear at all. By the time he's two years old, he's done a lot of chewing, and the milk teeth are worn down a bit. In the next year, the foal will get to be his full grown-up size. He'll also lose his two front teeth, top and bottom, and his permanent teeth will grow in their place. The permanent teeth are much bigger than the milk teeth, and when they first come in they have sharp edges and a dark mark on the chewing surface, which will eventually wear away. When Sophie's baby teeth fall out, the Tooth Fairy will probably bring her a quarter for each of them. That's what I got for mine. I don't know if there's a Tooth Fairy for horses. Probably not. Probably there isn't a Tooth Fairy for people either, but I'm afraid that if I tell Mom and Dad that, I'll stop getting money under my pillow. I'm too smart to blow a racket like that!

In the next year, the horse will lose four more baby teeth, two on the top, two on the bottom, on either side of the center teeth. When he's five, all the milk teeth will be gone, replaced by permanent teeth. A six-year-old horse shows wear on his center teeth. When he's seven, the four center teeth, top and bottom, will be noticeably worn. By the time he's eight, all his permanent teeth will be a little worn down, so that all the dark marks on the biting surface have disappeared.

After this, it gets a little hard to tell exactly how old a horse is because as they wear down, the teeth change shape. They become more triangular, with the flat side to the front and the points of the triangles toward the inside of the horse's mouth. The problem is that the rate of change isn't as predictable as it is before the horse is eight years old. By the time a horse is fifteen, all his teeth will be triangular, and by the time he's in his twenties, the teeth will be thicker than they are wide.

As Sophie gets older, I'll stop calling her a baby because she won't be one anymore. When she learns to walk she'll be a toddler, and when she can talk some and doesn't wobble so much when she walks, people

will call her a preschooler, then a kinder-
gartner, and so on. Eventually she'll be a
preteen, then a teenager, then a young
adult—well, you know how it goes. Horses
have different names at different ages, too.

For the first year, any horse can be called
a foal. If it's a boy, it can be called a colt foal.
A girl is a filly foal. You don't say "foal" anymore when it's a year old, so you just call it
a colt or a filly. You can also call it a yearling
then, but you continue to call it a colt or a
filly until it's full-grown. Then it's called a
pony or a horse. But things being the way
they are with horses and ponies, it's more
complicated than that! A female horse is
called a mare. A male horse is called a stallion. A stallion is very hard to ride because
he can be strong-willed and unpredictable.
An owner who wants to use a stallion for
riding usually has him neutered. Then he's
called a gelding.

Sophie will grow older, and so will I. And
no matter how old I get and how old she
gets, she's always going to be one very special thing to me—my little sister.

About the Author

Bonnie Bryant was born and raised in New York City, and she still lives there today. She spends her summers in a house on a lake in Massachusetts.

Ms. Bryant began writing about girls and horses when she started The Saddle Club in 1987. So far there are more than sixty books in that series. Much as she likes telling the stories about Stevie, Carole, and Lisa, she decided that the younger riders at Pine Hollow, especially May Grover, have stories of their own that need telling. That's how Pony Tails was born.

Ms. Bryant rides horses when she has time away from her computer, but she doesn't have a horse of her own. She likes to ride different horses and enjoys a variety of riding experiences. She says she thinks most of her readers are much better riders than she is!